An Apple a Day

An Apple a Day

From Orchard to You

Dorothy Hinshaw Patent

Photographs by
William Muñoz

Cobblehill Books/Dutton   New York

ACKNOWLEDGMENTS

The author and photographer want to thank Snokist Growers, Brad Tukey, Dick Zimmer, Diane Bilderback, Greg Patent, Art Callan, Michael Hofkins, and Albert and Wilma Park for their help with this book. Special thanks go to Nancy Callan for reading and commenting on the manuscript.

Library of Congress Cataloging-in-Publication Data
Patent, Dorothy Hinshaw.
An apple a day : from orchard to you / Dorothy Hinshaw Patent :
photographs by William Muñoz.
p.   cm.
Includes index.
Summary: An overview of growing apples, from planting and harvesting to
the grocery shelves.
ISBN 0-525-65020-2
1. Apple—Juvenile literature.   [1. Apple.   2. Apple industry.]
I. Muñoz, William, ill.   II. Title.
SB363.P34 1990   634'.11-dc20   89-33504   CIP   AC

Published in the United States by E.P. Dutton, New York, N.Y.,
a division of Penguin Books USA Inc.
Published simultaneously in Canada by Fitzhenry & Whiteside
Limited, Toronto.
Designer : Jean Krulis
Printed in Hong Kong
First edition
10 9 8 7 6 5 4 3 2 1

For my father,
H. Corwin Hinshaw,
who grew up with apples
and taught me how a ripe,
crisp apple should taste.

Contents

Michael enjoys a fresh, juicy apple.

1

Apples and More Apples

Biting into a crunchy, crisp apple is one of the joys of life. And who can resist the aroma of a juicy apple pie baking in the oven? Apples treat our taste buds in many ways. We drink apple juice when we are thirsty and eat applesauce with lunch. During the cold winter months, apples are one of the few fresh fruits we can enjoy. Not only do apples taste great, they are good for you. Apples contain lots of vitamin C, potassium, and fiber, all of which are important to your health.

How much do you know about this healthful, delicious fruit? Where are apples grown? How do they get from the grower to your grocery store? Why are they available all year around while most other fruits are not?

Apples have been eaten by people since before recorded history. They have been cultivated for so long that we don't know for sure just where they came from. Scientists think, however, that wild apples that grew in southwestern Asia were bred with one another to produce

9

improved, cultivated kinds. The art of growing and breeding apples was already being practiced by the ancient Greeks and Romans two thousand years ago. Even today, we eat some varieties that existed long ago. For example, Pippin apples were already popular in England over four hundred years ago.

AMERICA ADOPTS THE APPLE

Apples were brought to America by early European settlers. The seeds were especially easy to take along and produced a wide variety of trees when planted in the new land. The climate in the northern United States is perfect for growing apples, with hot, moist summers, crisp falls, and cold winters. While apple trees need warm, sunny weather to grow and produce fruit, they also require a certain amount of cold weather during the winter while they are resting in order to "wake up" and bloom in the springtime. Because they grew so well with little special care, apples were popular with the early Americans. The trees became quite large. But since settlers generally had plenty of land, almost anyone could grow an apple tree in the yard and harvest fruit that lasted through the long, frigid winter.

The spread of apples was aided by an unusual man

Wild apple trees like this one dot the farms and highways of America.

named John Chapman. He got the nickname "Johnny Appleseed" because he planted appleseeds and gave the young trees to settlers heading West. He was responsible for the planting of thousands of apple trees in Pennsylvania, Ohio, Indiana, and Illinois.

Apples were so identified with America that the phrase, "as American as apple pie," became an American motto. The most widely planted variety in the world today, the Delicious, originated in the United States. The United States is the world's biggest apple-producing country. More than 48 million apple trees grow in the United States, providing about 8.5 billion pounds of fruit each year!

KINDS OF APPLES

Grocery stores today only market a few types of apples. Six varieties—Delicious, McIntosh, Golden Delicious, Rome, Jonathan, and York—make up 80 percent of the U.S. crop. But there are actually thousands of kinds of apples, probably more varieties than any other fruit. There are over 150 strains of Delicious apples alone. Next time you go to the store, look carefully at the Delicious apples. Some will be deep, dark red, while others are lighter and have faint stripes running from the stem end

The popular Delicious apple got its start in the United States.

*Each apple in this bowl is a different variety, representing only a
tiny fraction of apples available today.*

around the sides. The pale ones are older strains, while the
dark ones are newer kinds. Try one of each type and see
which you like better.

Why are there so many varieties of apples? Harvesting
time is one reason. Some apples get ripe in the summer,
giving growers an early crop, while others must stay on
the tree until late fall to develop their full flavor. Lodi, one
of the earliest apples, is ready to pick about 75 days after
blooming. Granny Smith, on the other hand, takes 180
days to reach ripeness. Some of the newer strains of Delicious mature earlier than older ones. Now, instead of hav-
ing all the Delicious apples ripen at the same time,

growers can plant several types with different harvesting times. That way, they can harvest the orchard bit by bit, as each strain ripens in turn.

Climate also makes a big difference in growing apples. Some kinds, like Gravenstein, do well where winters are mild, like Northern California. Others, such as Northern Spy, are hardy enough to thrive in snowy, cold New England. But taste is probably the biggest reason for the multitude of apple varieties. While one person may enjoy the rich sweetness of a Red Delicious, another loves the tart crunch of a Granny Smith. Some of the best-tasting apples are not pretty to look at. Backyard gardeners are often happy to harvest such kinds and enjoy their special flavors, but shoppers are not likely to choose them. For this reason, you don't often see some of the tastiest varieties in the supermarket. Chances are you've never heard of the varieties Cox's Orange Pippin or Ashmead's Kernel. These are both tasty, old varieties, but unless you go to a store that features unusual produce, the apples you can buy are ones that look tempting to people who can't resist big, shiny, smooth-skinned fruit.

MAKING APPLE TREES

We usually think of growing plants from seeds. But trees from seeds may be very different from the parent since only pollen from a different variety can pollinate most kinds of apple. The seed from a Delicious, for example, may result in a tree with small, sour fruit. It will probably not be like a Delicious at all. So, fruit trees these days are pieced together at the nursery, not grown from seeds. To make a new tree that is just like its parent, the grower cuts off a slender shoot or a bud. The shoot or bud is then carefully pressed onto the cut trunk of a young tree with a thin trunk. The two pieces from the different trees are then tightly taped together. This is done during the dormant season when the plants have no leaves. The wood from the two plants grows together and produces a new tree.

BIG TREES, SMALL TREES

Backyard apple trees have always been favorites for climbing by children growing up in small towns. But big trees require a lot of space, and they take many years before bearing fruit. Most apple trees planted today will never grow big enough to climb. Now, anyone with a small bit of ground can grow fruit trees like apples and get a harvest in a few years. The trees stay small and produce early. You can buy an apple tree that will grow in a tub and never become taller than eight feet, or get one that reaches ten or twelve feet in height instead of the twenty or more feet of a full-sized tree.

The secret of controlling tree height lies in the roots. Some kinds of roots make for tall trees, while others produce short ones. While the tree itself never gets very big, it blooms and bears normal-sized fruit when only a few years old.

A bud grafted onto a rootstock, before being wrapped tightly in place. The tiny stick is actually the stem of a leaf which was cut off. The bud itself is at the base of the leaf.

This shoot sprouted from a graft onto the rootstock. It will grow into a new tree.

Full-sized apple trees are ideal for climbing but take up a lot of space.

Dwarf apple trees bear fruit while they are quite small.

Home growers and apple farmers alike love these small trees. Now a family can have half a dozen small trees of different varieties in the area once taken by one full-sized tree. The farmer gets several bonuses. He can harvest years earlier than before. The small trees come into peak production after only eight to ten years, while the big ones take fifteen to twenty years. The apples are much easier to harvest, too. Instead of using long, dangerous ladders, pickers can work from the ground and from short, sturdy ladders.

2

How Apples Grow

Have you ever wondered how an apple comes to be? How does a hard, woody tree produce a tender, juicy fruit? What are the steps that lead from a small, pinkish-white flower to a big, shiny apple?

BRANCHES AND SPURS

If you look at the branches of a tree, you will see that each larger branch gives off smaller ones at fairly regular intervals. After growing for awhile, the branch produces buds that grow into new branches. In a full-sized apple tree, the branches are much farther apart than they are in a dwarf tree.

Fruits like apples are produced on special branches called *spurs*. Instead of being inches or feet apart, the buds on spurs are very close together. Each year, the spur only grows a tiny bit before forming a new bud. The bud may be one that just produces leaves in the spring, or it can be one

21

These short side branches are called spurs. They produce blossoms in the springtime.

that develops into both leaves and flowers. Even after many years, a fruit spur is only a few inches long.

APPLE BLOSSOM TIME

An apple tree in full bloom is a glorious sight, with its bright green leaves and puffy white or pink flowers. Each flower has five delicate petals. If you look closely, you can see tiny stalks in the middle of the flower. In the very center are five white ones, surrounded by others with yellow tops. The white ones, which are hard to see, are called the *styles*. These are female parts of the flower. The ones with yellow tops are the male parts, called *stamens*. The yellow tops on the stamens are called *anthers*. The anthers

Apple blossoms. The stalks in this flower with the yellow tops are called stamens. They produce pollen.

produce pollen. When a bee comes to the flowers to collect pollen or sweet nectar, some of the pollen sticks to the hairs on its body. When the bee goes on to another flower, the pollen brushes off onto the tips of the styles, called the *stigmas,* of the other flower.

THE START OF AN APPLE

The pollen contains the sperm of the apple. When a grain of pollen lands on the stigma of another flower, it grows a long, tiny tube down through the style into the base of the flower. There lies the ovary, where the female

These tiny apples have just begun to grow.

Beehives can be moved so that the bees can pollinate different crops throughout the year.

eggs await fertilization. When the pollen tube reaches the ovary, the sperm cell inside is released and fertilizes one of the eggs. Eventually, the fertilized egg becomes a seed. Each apple flower has ten eggs in the ovary. If every one is fertilized, the resulting apple will have ten seeds.

The pollen from one variety of apple often won't be able to pollinate the flowers from the same variety. For this reason, apple growers must plant at least two varieties of apples in their orchards, close enough together that the bees will work both kinds of trees. Growers may use crab apple trees instead of another apple variety, which produce large numbers of flowers, to pollinate their apples. They also bring in portable beehives to make sure that there are enough bees around to give them a good crop.

TINY APPLES GROW

Getting from the pollinated flower to the ripe apple requires many different steps. Some of these involve *hormones*, special chemicals produced by the plant that have effects on the cells. If a flower isn't pollinated, it falls from the tree. But a pollinated flower stays and grows into a fruit, because a hormone is produced that prevents it from falling off.

For a month or more after pollination, the cells of the tiny apple grow and divide. Slowly, the fruit swells and begins to look more and more like an apple. Since the fruit cells come from the female parent, it doesn't matter what variety provided the pollen. All the fruit on one tree will be the same variety, even though the seeds they carry are different.

As the apples grow, there are two times when some of the developing fruit may drop off the tree. Some fall soon after pollination, while others drop later, in June. The apples that survive grow steadily to their final sizes. One hormone that helps the apple grow is made by the seeds. If the flower wasn't completely pollinated, fewer than ten seeds result. The apple is lopsided, because the flesh over the seedless part doesn't grow as much as the rest. But growing is not the only part of becoming a sweet, juicy fruit. If you've ever picked unripe apples and bitten into them, you know that they are tough and very sour.

The little apples grow throughout the summer, looking more and more like apples all the time.

WHEN ARE THEY RIPE?

Ripening involves several processes. The tough flesh is transformed into pleasantly crunchy, juicy fruit. In the unripe apple, the cells have hard walls around them. As the fruit ripens, these walls are dissolved, and air is brought in. Twenty-five percent of the flesh of a ripe apple is actually air. Really big apples may have extra air and therefore less flavor.

During ripening, the starch in the unripe fruit is changed into sweet sugar, and many special chemicals are manufactured that give each variety its unique flavor. While all these activities proceed inside the fruit, the green chlorophyll in the skin disappears as red or yellow pigments are produced.

Apple farmers need ways to tell when their crops are at the peak of ripeness. Figuring this out is not always easy. For one thing, fruit on different parts of the tree may not ripen at the same time. The apples that are exposed to the sun can be ready to eat before those in the cool, shady inside of the tree. Once, you could tell by the color of the fruit when it was ripe. But the newer strains of highly colored apples look bright and rosy before the flesh inside has developed its full flavor.

One way to tell if the fruit is ready is to pick a sample. The apple is cut, and a solution of iodine is dropped on the cut surface. If there is still starch in the apple, the iodine turns blue. Then the farmer knows to wait before harvesting the crop. Since apples become soft as they reach ripeness, a machine that puts pressure on the fruit and measures its hardness can also give clues as to the best time to pick. Varieties such as McIntosh are ripe when their seeds turn brown.

You can tell which one of these apples is ripe by the color of the seeds.

3

At the Orchard

Even with today's smaller trees that produce fruit earlier, running an apple orchard takes patience and hard work. The grower still must wait years after planting to get a good crop. During all that time, he or she must take good care of them so that they will be healthy and strong.

SHAPING THE TREES

Young fruit trees need more than sunshine, water, and good soil. In order to grow well and give good, well-colored fruit, the trees must be shaped as they grow. The green chlorophyll in the leaves takes energy from the sunlight and stores it as sugar. The sugar is used by the tree to produce and grow fruit. For this reason, the more sunlight that reaches the leaves, the better the tree will grow and the more fruit it will produce. In order to open up the trees to the sunlight, fruit growers remove some branches. This trimming is called *pruning*. Branches that point toward

Strong clippers are used to prune fruit trees.

The cuts from pruning heal over as the tree grows.

the center of the tree are cut off. Ones that are growing outward are left on the tree. Pruning can also help keep the height of the trees under control by trimming branches that point upward.

Pruning is usually done in late winter, while the trees are dormant. There is little other work at that time, and when the trees begin to grow again in a few weeks, the wounds will heal over.

SPRINGTIME IN THE ORCHARD

The most critical time for apple growers is the spring. When the trees start to bloom, the grower must make sure there are enough bees. One or two hives for every acre of orchard are brought in to help pollinate the flowers. Each hive has about 60,000 willing worker bees ready to collect pollen and nectar. Everyone hopes for warm, sunny weather during blossoming so that the bees will work hard and do a good job of pollination.

During blossom time and for a couple of weeks afterwards, fruit growers worry about frost. If apple flowers or young fruit freeze, the crop will be lost. Growers have alarms connected to thermometers that will go off if frost threatens and temperatures fall below 36° F. Then everyone in the family gets up, no matter what the hour, and works to save the crop. Some orchards have giant fans that

An orchard in bloom is heaven for bees.

blow the cold air away so it won't settle in the orchard. Orchard pots in which fires burn to heat the air also help. Sometimes just turning on the sprinklers and keeping the trees wet can keep the frost away. Once the unpredictable spring weather is over and a good set of fruit has formed, the grower can rest more easily.

When frost hasn't ruined the crop, too many apples often develop on the tree. Even though some drop off in June, the trees can still carry too much fruit for their own good. It takes the energy collected by thirty to forty leaves to ripen one big, sweet apple. The apples on a tree with excess fruit will be small, and the tree can put so much energy into them that it won't give a good crop the next year. For this reason, orchardists often must thin their crop in the early summer. Some orchards are thinned by spraying chemicals that make some of the fruit fall off. But thinning by hand gives more control of the crop. Workers pick off all but two or three apples in a cluster and leave some spurs free of fruit so that they will produce flower buds the next year.

BATTLING PESTS

Apples can be attacked by several pests and diseases. The most common is the codling moth, which is respon-

Apple trees naturally drop some excess fruit from their branches in June.

There are too many apples in this cluster, so it needs to be thinned.

The same cluster after thinning.

sible for wormy apples. The adult is a small, grayish brown moth that blends in with tree bark. The moth lays its eggs at the blossom end of very young apples. When a tiny caterpillar hatches, it burrows inside the fruit. There it lives and grows until the fall. Then it tunnels out of the apple and heads for the bark, where it spins a cocoon and waits out the winter. In the spring, the moths come out, mate, and begin the cycle over again.

Tent caterpillars are one pest of fruit growers.

Other insects also bother apples. Leaf rollers eat the leaves or fruit. In a bad year, leaf rollers can seriously damage the crop, either by consuming all the leaves on the trees or by eating the fruit. Aphids are small insects that suck the juices from plants. They can damage the young fruit, too.

Fire blight is one of the most serious apple diseases. It is caused by bacteria that enter the trees through the flowers, young branches, or damaged parts of the bark. The disease is called fire blight because the infected area of the tree turns black and looks as if it has been burned.

Because of these and other pests, apple growers spray their crops several times during the growing season. Different chemicals are used, depending on which pests and diseases are a problem in the orchard. Because spraying is expensive and because some people worry about the effects of the chemicals on people, scientists are working hard on developing trees that can resist diseases.

HARVESTING THE CROP

Watering, spraying, and watching out for problems keep the apple grower busy all spring and summer. Harvesttime begins when the first variety in the orchard is ripe. The grower must get enough pickers for his crop. Some will be local people. But others are professionals who spend their lives on the move, traveling from south to north with the ripening fruit crops.

Picking apples is hard work. Since pickers are paid by

Fire blight is a serious disease of apples.

the amount of fruit they collect rather than by the hour, they get very good at working quickly. Still, the pickers must be careful when removing the fruit. It is important to pick the stem but not damage the vital spur. Without the spurs, there would be no fruit.

In the old days, the apples were collected in sturdy bushel baskets. The baskets were collected from the fields, and the fruit was sold to stores by the bushel. Then, apples were a seasonal crop, only available for a few weeks after harvest. Today, however, the picked fruit goes through many stages before it reaches the supermarket produce counter, and it may not get there until many months after being picked.

Picking apples.

4

From Tree to Market

The Yakima Valley of Washington State is a prime fruit-growing region. Washington grows more apples than any other state, and "Washington State apples" are famous around the country for their quality. Most growers in the area have about twenty-five acres of orchard, not enough to market their own apples. The growers generally get together into co-ops. Their crops are pooled to make packing and selling the fruit more efficient. Snokist Growers in Yakima is one of the three largest co-ops in the state. Once the apples have been picked, the co-op takes care of sorting, storing, packing, and selling the apples for the growers.

The bins of apples from the orchard are brought to the sorting and packing plant by truck. Each bin contains apples grown in one orchard. While there is usually only one variety in each bin, perfect bright red or golden fruit shares the space with scarred, poorly colored apples, so the fruit must be sorted.

QUALITY COUNTS

At Snokist, which has a typical processing plant, two separate operations take place. First the apples are removed from the bins and sorted by size and grade. The sorted apples are put back into bins and stored in the cold before being cleaned and packed in boxes to be shipped. That way, when a big order comes in for a certain size and grade of apple, it can be filled easily by removing fruit of the desired type from storage and packing it. Plants that

At the sorting plant, bins of apples are lifted before the fruit is floated out.

pack the fruit right after sorting don't have enough fruit of the same size and grade at one time to fill a big order.

As anyone who has ever bobbed for apples knows, apples float on water. Packers take advantage of this trait and use water to move apples through the plant gently. Each bin is submerged, and the apples float out. The water carrying the apples moves around to the first sorting machine, called the eliminator chain. The eliminator chain is wire mesh through which very small fruit falls. These tiny apples, called *chops*, are too tiny for anything but juice, so they are sent to a juice factory.

The rest of the apples are delivered by a conveyor belt to human sorters who examine them for flaws. Most of the fruit is divided into two grades, Fancy and Extra Fancy. The differences between the two are based on how the apples look, not on how ripe or tasty they are. Extra Fancy apples have good color, even shapes, and no surface blemishes. Fancy fruit may not be quite as well colored. It may have small bruises or marks, and it may be uneven in shape. The sorters look for all the flaws except color. They place apples with many flaws, called processors, on one conveyor belt. The processors become applesauce and apple slices for pies. The Fancys are put on another belt, while the Extra Fancys are left alone.

The apples float through the sorting plant.

Sorters place the processor apples on the conveyor belt. You can see the flaws in these apples.

MEASURING COLOR AND SIZE

Next, a machine takes over and sorts the apples for color and size. First, they pass under a light. The darker its color, the less light each apple reflects. Thus, the most highly colored fruit reflects the least light. Next, each

The apples are spread out so that each is in its own compartment.

piece of fruit is then quickly weighed and dumped into an individual plastic cup. A computer keeps track of the color and weight measurement for each apple. Under the moving rows of cups are troughs of water, a different trough for each size and grade of fruit. As an apple passes over the trough which carries apples of its size and grade, the cup releases and drops the apple into the water.

Now the time has come to put the apples back into bins to await packing. Each trough leads to a loading spot, where a bin awaits underwater. The computer knows how many apples of a particular size it takes to fill a bin. It also remembers how many apples of that size have been dumped into the trough. When the right number of apples has collected in the water over the submerged bin, a light goes on. This tells a human operator that it is time to fill the bin. The operator pushes a button, and the bin is lifted under the floating apples. The water drains out through the cracks, and the apples are ready to be stored.

The filled bins are taken by forklifts into a huge cold storage room, where they are stacked to await final packing into boxes. Temperatures in the 30s keep the apples fresh for a few weeks. If they must be stored longer, they are placed into controlled atmosphere storage, called just CA.

SUSPENDED FRESHNESS

CA counts on the fact that apples are living things, even though they have been removed from the trees. Each

Enough apples have collected to fill a bin.

fruit takes in oxygen from the air and uses it to stay alive. Oxygen is also involved in the ripening process. The warmer the fruit is, the faster it uses oxygen, and the faster it ripens. Cold air helps slow the ripening process down, but it doesn't stop it. If you leave apples in the refrigerator, they will stay fresh for some time. But eventually they would become overripe.

The key to CA is lowering the oxygen content of the air. Air normally contains about 20 percent oxygen. By

Apples "breathe" through the tiny light spots in the skin.

reducing the oxygen to about 2 percent and keeping the temperature at 31° to 32° F., CA puts the apples to sleep. They have enough oxygen to stay alive but not enough to ripen any further. Carbon dioxide given off by the fruit also helps keep the fruit from ripening anymore. In CA, the humidity is kept at about 95 percent, which keeps the fruit from drying out. If people need to enter the room, they must wear masks and carry oxygen tanks with them. Even after months in CA, an apple can be as crisp and fresh-tasting as it was the day after picking.

Shiny Red Apples

When it is time to pack the apples for shipment, they are taken to the packing plant and floated out of the bins. They are soaped and brushed to clean them. Then they are

The soapy apples are gently turned to help clean them; then they are rinsed off.

They are sprayed with a thin coating of wax.

rinsed in hot water and dried by rollers and a fan blowing
warm air. When they are completely dry, the apples are
coated with a thin film of hot wax and dried in a heat
tunnel. Now they are shiny and bright, ready to be eaten.

The waxed apples get one last check to make sure no
fruit of the wrong grade or size sneaked through the sys-
tem. Workers then pack the fruit carefully into boxes,
which are closed and stamped with the size of the apples.
Each box holds forty to forty-two pounds of apples, the
equivalent of the old-time bushel.

Finally, perhaps months after being picked from the
tree, the crisp, juicy apples are on their way to the supermarket, where we can buy them for our own enjoyment
and health.

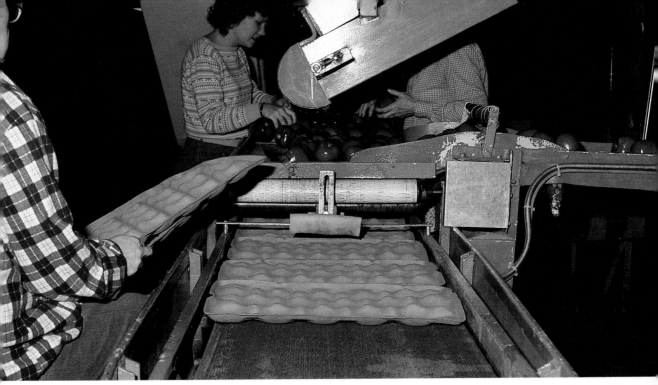

The layers of apples in the boxes are cushioned for protection.

The boxes are weighed to make sure they are full.

5

The Versatile Apple

While crunchy raw apples are a delight, apples are also tasty fixed in other ways. The apples rejected for fresh use at the packing plant are turned into refreshing juice, tasty sauce, or other apple products. And some apples are raised specially for making cider. Altogether, about half the apples grown in the United States are turned into frozen, canned, or baked products.

JUICE AND CIDER

Apple juice and sweet cider are both made by simply pressing the liquid from apples. Since apples are 87 percent water, they give plenty of juice. Apple juice is filtered and treated to turn it into a clear, amber fluid. It is pasteurized by heating to 170° F., to kill any bacteria that

Wild apples like these are perfect for making cider.

might spoil it. Then it is sealed into cans or bottles for sale. Unfiltered juice is sometimes available as well.

Traditional apple cider is a fresh product, available only at harvesttime. But nowadays, pasteurized and bottled "cider" is also available which is very similar to apple juice.

The best cider comes either from special cider apple varieties or by mixing different varieties together. Tart kinds, such as Jonathans or Winesaps, are combined with sweet ones, like Golden Delicious, and mixed with fragrant varieties, like McIntosh or Gravenstein. Throwing in a few crab apples adds extra zing to the brew. Juice and cider are made the same way, whether in a big factory or at home. The fruit is cut up into small pieces and the juice squeezed out, leaving behind the peel and pulp.

Many people feel that pasteurization damages the flavor of apple cider, so they look forward to fall, when they can buy it fresh. Fresh cider that is made carefully and cleanly will keep for a week or two in a refrigerator. If left longer, it will ferment, resulting in a liquid that is at first bubbly and tangy but eventually alcoholic. Hard cider, also called applejack, is the result of such apple cider fermentation.

Dick Zimmer uses a homemade cider press. The apples are loaded into the top. A rotating bar covered with nails cuts them into pulp. You can see the pulp entering the press from the chute.

You can buy many different apple products in the grocery store.

APPLESAUCE

Another tasty way to use imperfect fruit is to make applesauce. This tasty food is a simple combination of cooked apples and sugar, sometimes with some cinnamon added. If the peels are left on the fruit, a pleasantly pink sauce results. Canning companies usually use a mixture of four or five varieties to make their sauce. That way, when one variety becomes unavailable, they can substitute another without drastically changing the taste and color of the sauce.

As Dick tightens the top pressing down on the apples, cider flows from the press into a bucket.

61

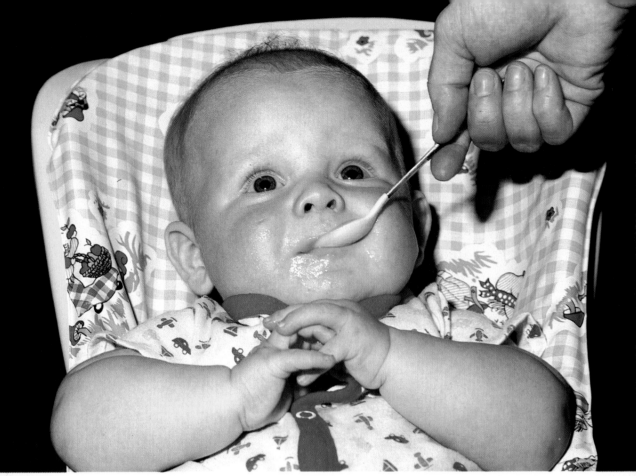

Sean may make a mess, but he enjoys eating his applesauce.

COOKING WITH APPLES

Apple pie is an American favorite, along with such tasty treats as baked apples and apple crisp. Some varieties that are wonderful for fresh eating are not good for cooking. They aren't tart enough or don't have a firm enough texture for baking. Golden Delicious is probably the best all-around apple, because it is good to eat both fresh and cooked. York, Jonathan, Stayman, Rome

Beauty, Granny Smith, and McIntosh all can make delicious baked goods. The popular Red Delicious, however, isn't tart enough to make a good cooking apple.

THE VERSATILE FRUIT

Altogether, it is easy to see why apples are a favorite American fruit. Their delicious flavor, easy keeping, and variety of uses make them perhaps the most versatile of all fruits.

Everyone loves apple pie. Here is one ready to eat.